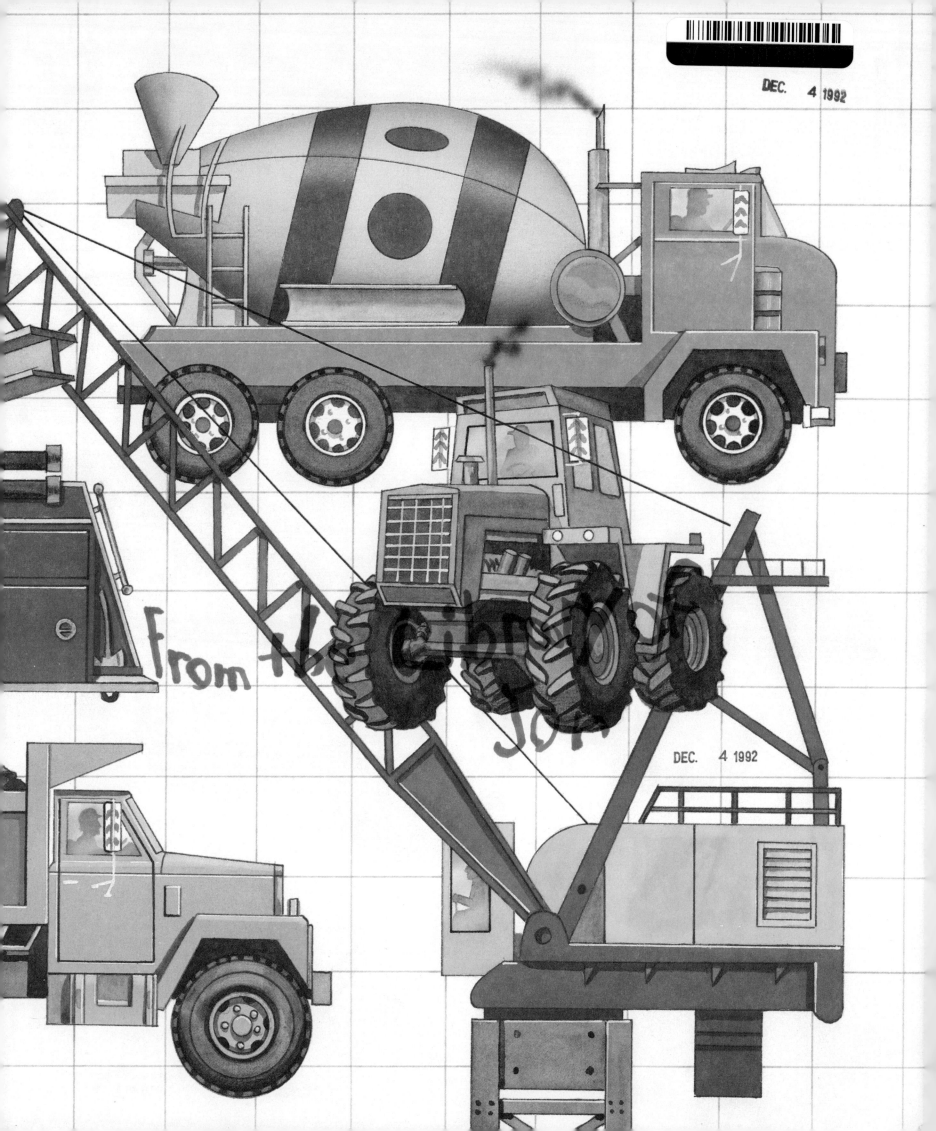

This book
belongs to
Jon Parker

Giant Work Machines

By Thea Feldman
Illustrated by Tom LaPadula

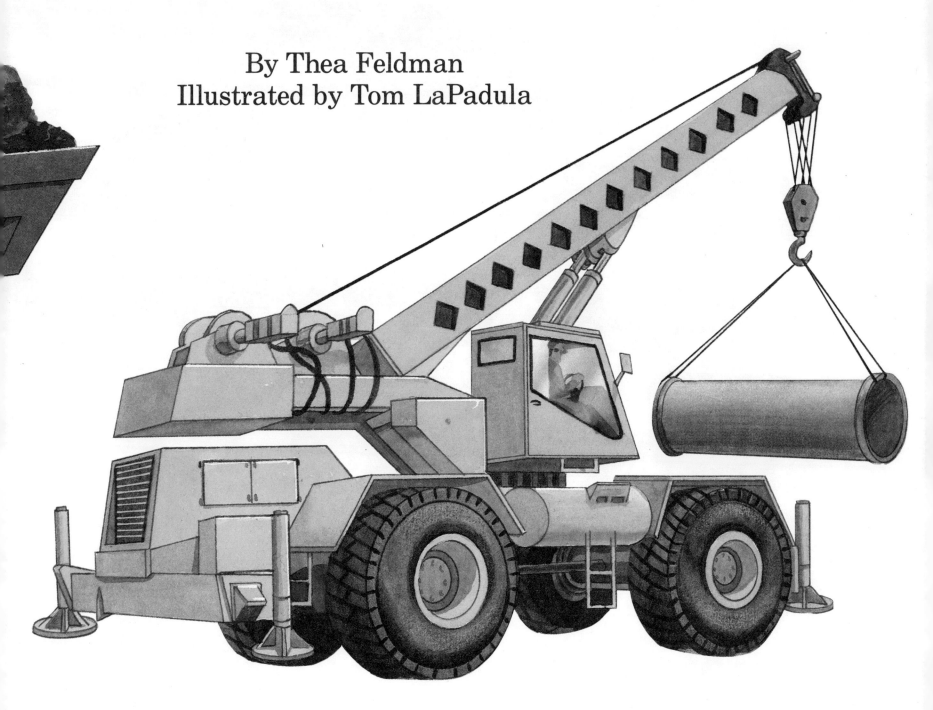

A GOLDEN BOOK • NEW YORK
Western Publishing Company, Inc., Racine, Wisconsin 53404

steamroller

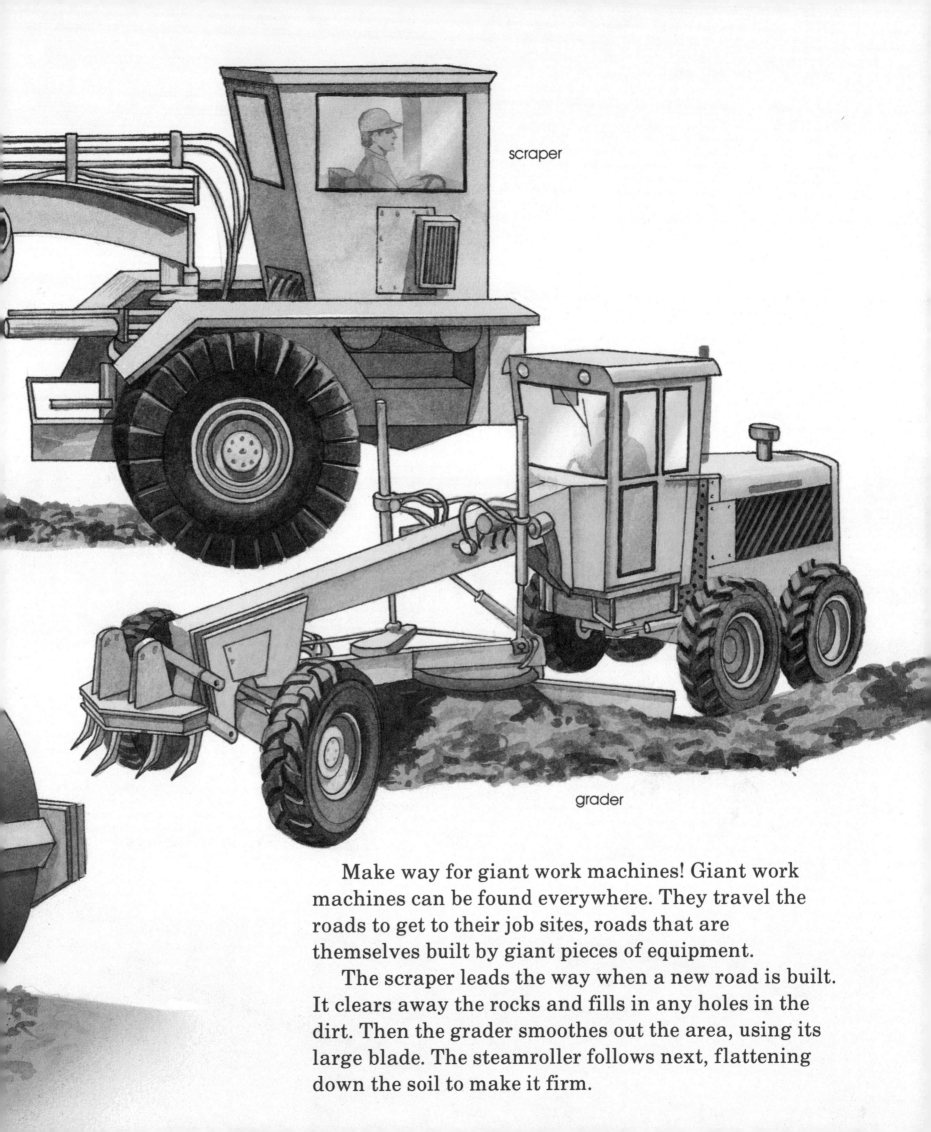

scraper

grader

Make way for giant work machines! Giant work machines can be found everywhere. They travel the roads to get to their job sites, roads that are themselves built by giant pieces of equipment.

The scraper leads the way when a new road is built. It clears away the rocks and fills in any holes in the dirt. Then the grader smoothes out the area, using its large blade. The steamroller follows next, flattening down the soil to make it firm.

Once the steamroller has done its job, wet concrete is poured on the soil and a paver rides slowly over it. The paver spreads the mass of concrete evenly.

The concrete road will be too smooth for cars and trucks to ride on without skidding. A machine called a finisher does the important job of making the new road rough enough for cars to pass over safely.

But the new road will not be ready for cars and
trucks until the line painter's work is done. This big
machine paints the lines that tell drivers which lanes
to drive in. Once the lines are dry, the new road can be
opened!

A heavy winter snowfall, however, can cover a road
so deeply that it is forced to close until a giant
snowplow arrives on the scene. Its whirring ribbon
blades clear away the mounds of snow, and the road
can then be opened again.

All roads and streets need to be kept clean. The street sweeper takes care of this with its big bushy brushes.

It is important that roadways are kept clear and clean so that other giant work machines can get to their jobs. Brightly colored fire engines go racing down the street when a fire has been reported. The pumper carries the hose that will be hooked up to a fire hydrant's water supply. And the hook and ladder truck carries the tall ladder that helps fire fighters reach high places.

Big fire-fighting trucks can also be found at the airport, where the fast-moving crash truck speeds to the scene of a plane crash or a fire. Another fire-fighting machine, the fireboat, works on land or in the water to protect seaports and shorelines.

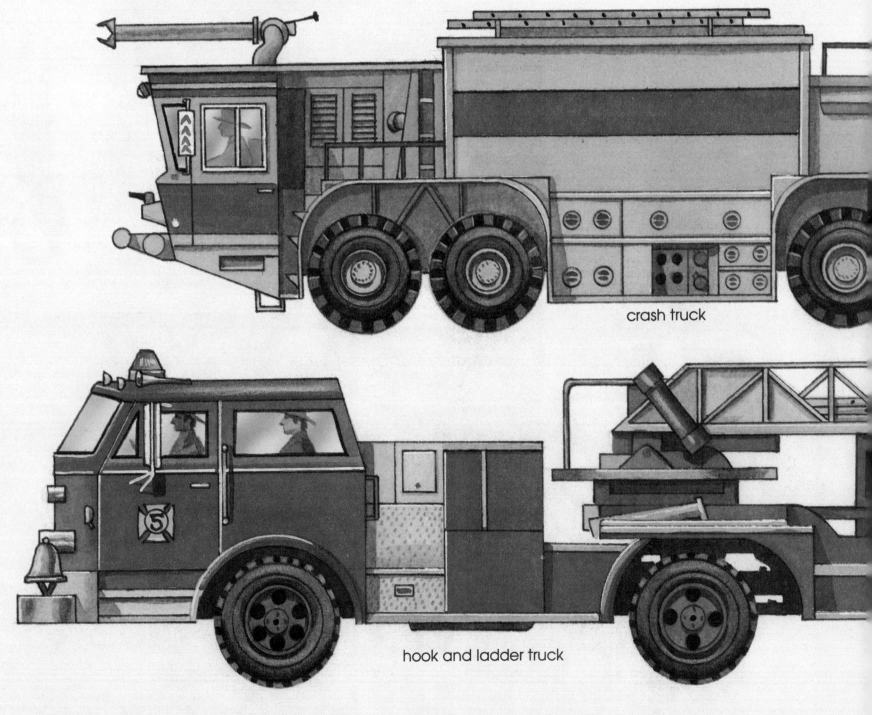

crash truck

hook and ladder truck

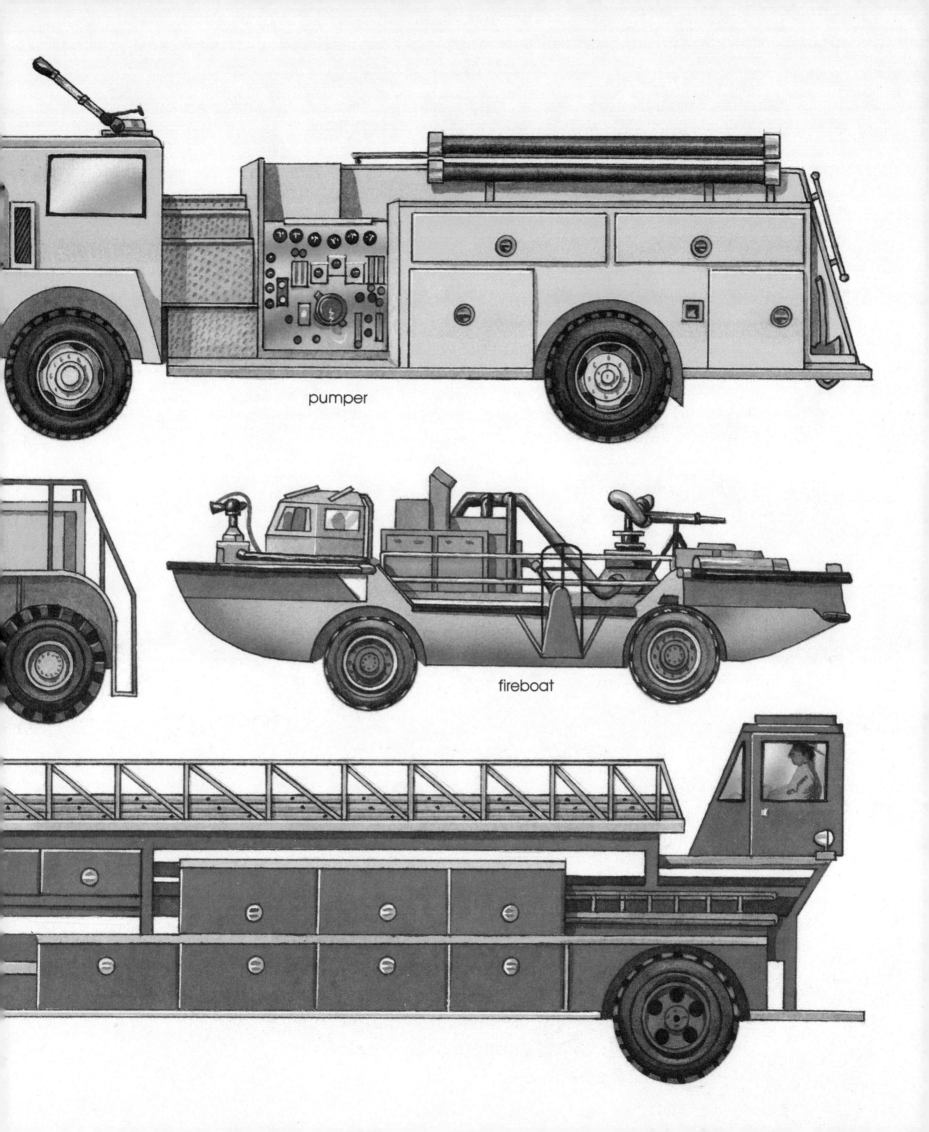

pumper

fireboat

Many giant work machines are found in cities, where they help build the buildings that people live and work in. Sometimes an old building stands in the place where a new building is supposed to go. A heavy steel wrecking ball, attached to a long crane, is called in to knock the old building down so that work may begin on the new one.

A dump truck carries pieces of the fallen building away and unloads them at a dump site. The driver makes the big bed tip back to get rid of its load. Dump trucks carry many things that do not need to be placed gently on the ground.

Back at the building site the mighty bulldozer chugs along, pushing piles of rocks and dirt out of the way with its heavy steel blades.

A front-end loader scoops the rocks and dirt up in its bucket. It will carry its load to a dump truck, waiting to take it away.

Once the dump truck, the bulldozer, and the front-end loader have cleared the area, a huge machine called an excavator digs the hole that will be the new building's foundation. Its clawlike steel shovel works fast and powerfully, creating new piles of rocks and dirt for the other big machines to remove.

A building's foundation helps support the weight of
that building. A gigantic pile driver hammers long
thin pieces of steel called piles into the hole made by
the excavator. The piles will be a firm support for the
rest of the building.

Once a foundation is finished, workers spread a smooth, thick layer of concrete over it. Concrete is sand, water, and cement mixed together in the huge slowly turning drum of a concrete mixer. The drum is always turning, and when it is needed, fresh concrete is sent pouring down a long chute at the back of the concrete mixer.

A trencher has a large round blade with sharp steel teeth. The blade cuts through streets and concrete sidewalks. Trenchers make deep narrow ditches for the water and gas pipes and electrical cables that will lead to the new building.

Many different types of cranes are found at building sites, doing a variety of jobs. Cranes are used to lift and move big heavy objects, such as the pipes that will go in the ditches made by the trencher.

Other cranes are used to lift steel beams and girders
up to building workers. A tower crane is a very tall
crane that can reach the highest part of a skyscraper.
Some cranes are attached to trucks. Others, like the
tower crane, stand by themselves.

tractor and plow

Big work machines are also found on farms. The most important farm machine is the tractor, because several different planting tools can be hooked to its back. First the tractor pulls a plow to get the soil ready for planting. Then the seed drill is hooked up to its back to plant the seeds and cover them. As the seeds grow into crops farmers ride their tractors through their fields while pulling a cultivator, a machine that uproots weeds.

When it is time to harvest the crops, a huge cutting machine called a combine is called in. Not only does the combine cut the plants, it takes out the seeds and grains and collects them in a special bin. The parts of the plants that are not needed are left behind on the ground.

Even more powerful work machines than those found on farms can be found in forests, cutting down thick trees. The wood from the trees is needed to build houses and to make paper, furniture, and many other things. A logging machine, or log feller, grips a tree and slices through its trunk with a huge strong blade. A skidder drags the tree logs away.

Big work machines are also found at harbors,
where a tall gantry crane shovels sand onto ships that
will carry it away. Gantry cranes also unload heavy
boxes from cargo ships. The legs of the machine are
spread wide apart so that other work machines can
drive through them to do their jobs.

Once the gantry crane has placed all the ship's boxes on shore, a strong forklift slides its platform under each box and carries it safely to the harbor's warehouse. Forklifts stack the boxes one on top of the other or on shelves. They can reach almost 40 feet high.

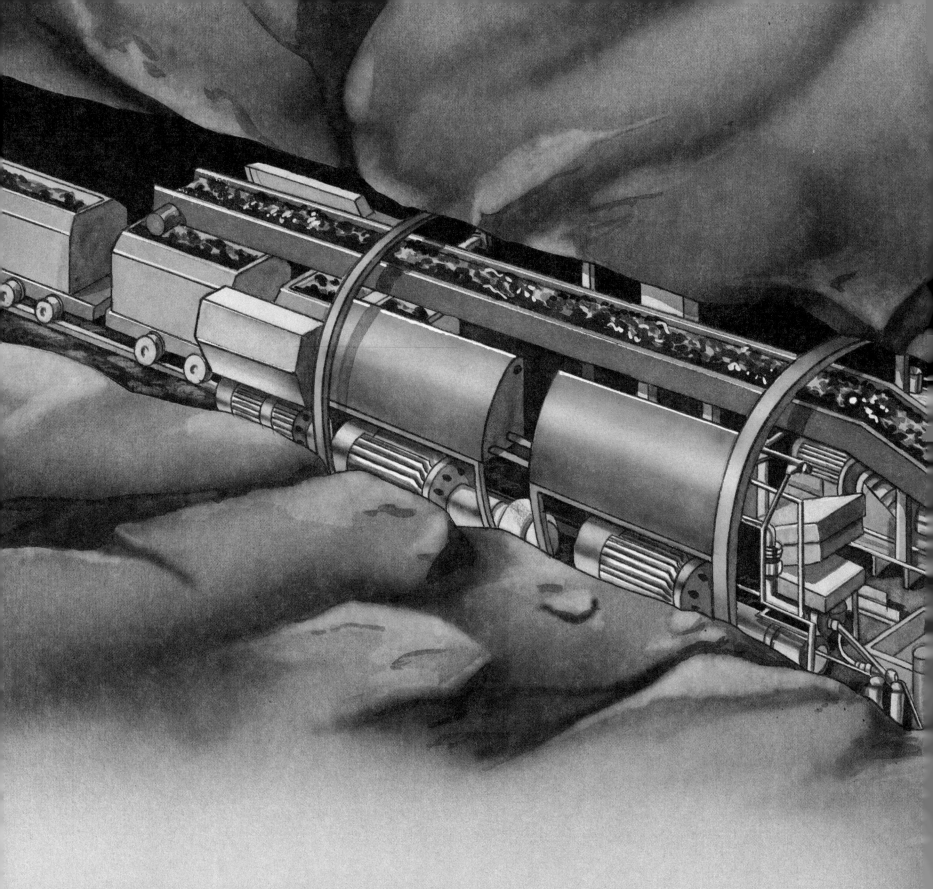

Giant machines do their jobs not only on the surface of the earth, but they can also be found hard at work deep in the ground. A tunnel-boring machine, or mole, slowly cuts through tough rock with dozens of small spinning blades.

The rocks and dirt are fed into little train cars
by a moving belt in the mole. The train goes back
to the surface, while the mole moves forward.

Another big machine that works below the surface
of the earth is the continuous miner, used for mining
coal. Once a passage has been dug, the continuous
miner rips coal out of the mine's wall with its turning
blades.

As the miner digs out the coal it is loaded into a shuttle car. Like the mole's train, the shuttle car goes back to the surface with its load.

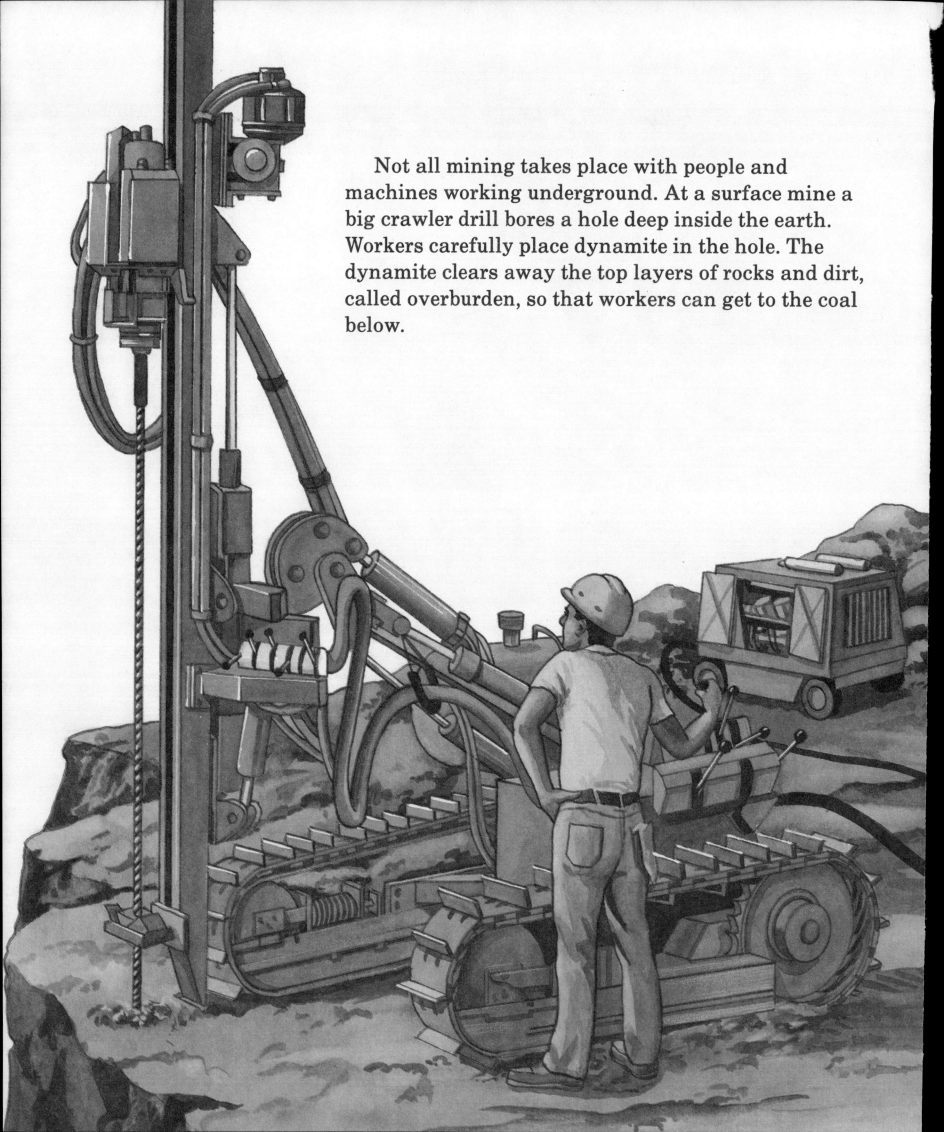

Not all mining takes place with people and machines working underground. At a surface mine a big crawler drill bores a hole deep inside the earth. Workers carefully place dynamite in the hole. The dynamite clears away the top layers of rocks and dirt, called overburden, so that workers can get to the coal below.

A power shovel will dig into the mounds of rocks
and dirt and lift them out of the way. Power shovels
can also break through the sides of mountains with
their sharp teeth to get to any minerals hidden there.

An enormous work machine called a dragline has a
huge bucket that scoops up overburden quickly.
Because its bucket is so big, the dragline is the fastest
way to get rid of overburden. The bucket swings down
from a high crane and attacks the earth.

Giant work machines can truly be found everywhere. Not only are they busy building roads or at work in cities, on farms, in forests, at the waterfront, underground, and at mining sites, but they are also found high above the earth, hard at work in outer space. Scenes like this might exist in the future. Giant work machines will always be on the job!

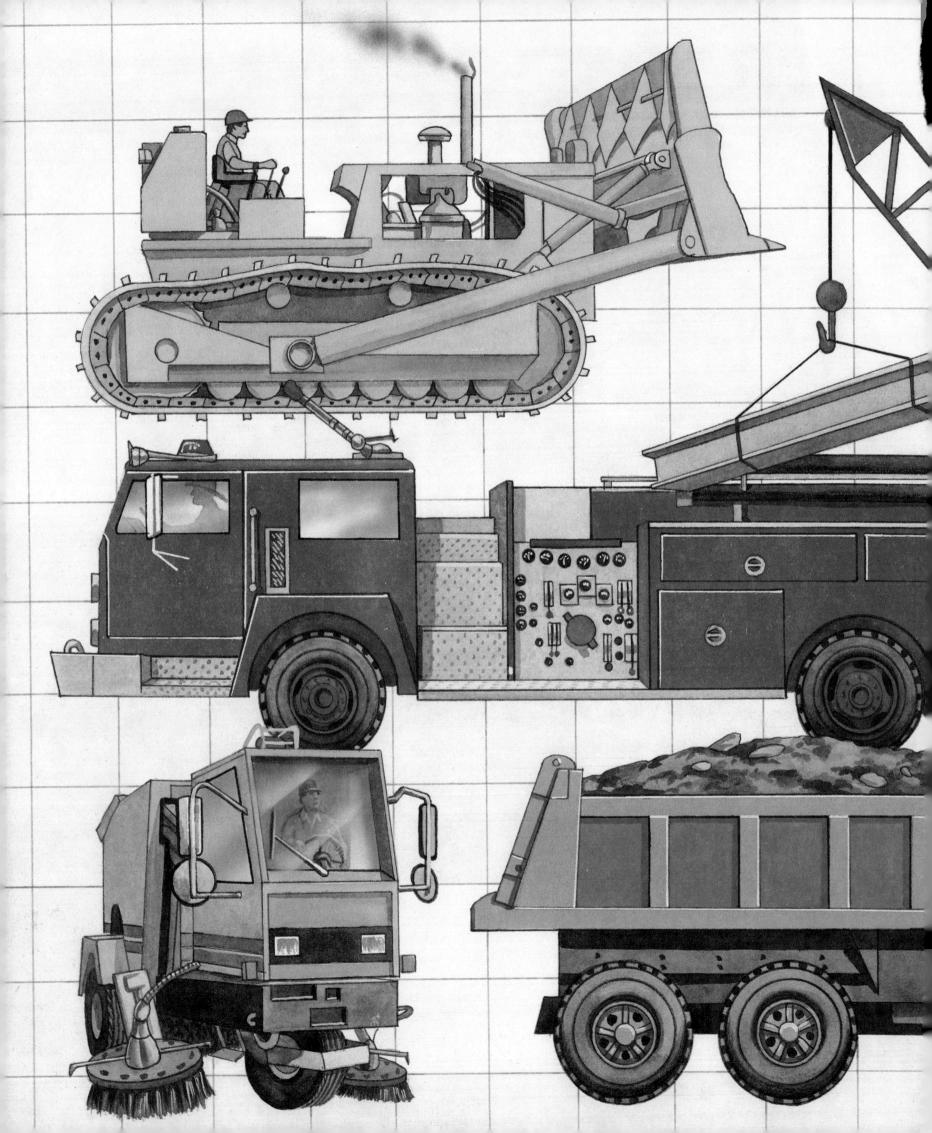